William Butler

Yeats

SELECTED POEMS

COMPILED BY

PATRICIA MOORE

UNABRIGED & COMPLETE

LONG READING TEXT

NEW DELHI (INDIA)

William Butler
Yeats
SELECTED
POEMS

This English Edition, Published in India

Published by

MG BOOKS

An Imprint of

MAANU GRAPHICS

MAANU GRAPHICS
(PUBLISHERS OF GENERAL BOOKS)
5FF, Ganpati Bhawan, 21 Ansari Road,
Darya Ganj, New Delhi-110002
Ph: 43755225, 9315898404
E-mail : maanugraphics@yahoo.com
mgbooks.maanu@yahoo.com

Printed at
Satyam Enterprises, Delhi

CONTENTS

About the Author

William Butler Yeats (1865-1939) was born in Dublin into an Irish Protestant family. His father, John Butler Yeats, a clergyman's son, was a lawyer turned to an Irish Pre-Raphaelite painter. Yeats's mother, Susan Pollexfen, came from a wealthy family - the Pollexfens had a prosperous milling and shipping business.

In 1881 the family returned to Dublin. While studying at the Metropolitan School of Art, Yeats met there the poet, dramatist, and painter George Russell (1867-1935). He was interested in mysticism, and his search inspired also Yeats. In 1886 Yeats formed the Dublin Lodge of the Hermetic Society and took the magical name Daemon est Deus Inversus. The occult order also attracted Aleister Crowley.

As a writer Yeats made his debut in 1885, when he published his first poems in The Dublin University Review. In 1887 the family returned to Bedford Park, and Yeats devoted himself to writing.

In 1889 Yeats met his great love, Maud Gonne (1866-1953), an an actress and Irish revolutionary who became a major landmark in the poets life and imagination. Yeats worshipped Maud, whom he wrote many poems. She married in 1903 Major John MacBride, and this episode inspired Yeats's poem 'No Second Troy'.

In 1896 Yeats returned to live permanently in his home country. He reformed Irish Literary Society, and then the National Literary Society in Dublin, which aimed to promote the New Irish Library.

Ezra Pound, whom Yeats met in 1912, became his fencing master and secretary in the winters of 1913 and 1914. Pound introduced Yeats to Japanese Noah drama, which inspired his plays. In early 1917 Yeats bought Thoor Ballyle, a derelict Norman stone tower near Coole Park. After restoring it, the tower became his summer home and central symbol in his later poetry.

At the age of 52, in 1917, he married Georgie Hyde-Lee, who was 26. Although Keats first had his doubts, the marriage was happy and they had a son and a daughter. During their honeymoon Yeats's wife demonstrated her gift for automatic writing. Their collaborative notebooks formed the basis of A VISION (1925), a book of marriage therapy spiced with occultism.

The change from suggestive, beautiful lyricism toward the spare and tragic bitterness was marked in Yeats poem 'September 1913' in which he stated: "Romantic Ireland's dead and gone."

THE WILD SWANS AT COOLE (1917) was set on the Coole Park, the estate of Yeats's friend and patron Lady Augusta Gregory. Yeats registers the death of Robert Gregory, Lady Gregory's son, and Mabel Beardley, sister of the English artist Aubrey Beardsley. The tone of the work is reflective, almost conversational, and occasionally the poet lets loose his bitterness and grief of the past. Yeats also returns to his relationship with Maud Gonne, who rejected his love.

In 1932 Yeats founded the Irish Academy of Letters and in 1933 he was briefly involved with the fascist Blueshirts in Dublin. While in Mallorca Yeats became seriously ill. He tried to meet Robert Graves who refused to see him. Yeats died in 1939 at the Hôtel Idéal Séjour, in Menton, France.

THE TOWER

I

What shall I do with this absurdity -
O heart, O troubled heart - this caricature,
Decrepit age that has been tied to me
As to a dog's tail?
Never had I more
Excited, passionate, fantastical
Imagination, nor an ear and eye
That more expected the impossible -
No, not in boyhood when with rod and fly,
Or the humbler worm, I climbed Ben Bulben's back
And had the livelong summer day to spend.
It seems that I must bid the Muse go pack,
Choose Plato and Plotinus for a friend
Until imagination, ear and eye,
Can be content with argument and deal
In abstract things; or be derided by
A sort of battered kettle at the heel.

II

I pace upon the battlements and stare
On the foundations of a house, or where
Tree, like a sooty finger, starts from the earth;
And send imagination forth
Under the day's declining beam, and call
Images and memories
From ruin or from ancient trees,
For I would ask a question of them all.

Beyond that ridge lived Mrs. French, and once
When every silver candlestick or sconce
Lit up the dark mahogany and the wine.
A serving-man, that could divine
That most respected lady's every wish,
Ran and with the garden shears
Clipped an insolent farmer's ears
And brought them in a little covered dish.

Some few remembered still when I was young
A peasant girl commended by a Song,
Who'd lived somewhere upon that rocky place,
And praised the colour of her face,
And had the greater joy in praising her,

Remembering that, if walked she there,
Farmers jostled at the fair
So great a glory did the song confer.

And certain men, being maddened by those rhymes,
Or else by toasting her a score of times,
Rose from the table and declared it right
To test their fancy by their sight;
But they mistook the brightness of the moon
For the prosaic light of day -
Music had driven their wits astray -
And one was drowned in the great bog of Cloone.

Strange, but the man who made the song was blind;
Yet, now I have considered it, I find
That nothing strange; the tragedy began
With Homer that was a blind man,
And Helen has all living hearts betrayed.
O may the moon and sunlight seem
One inextricable beam,
For if I triumph I must make men mad.

And I myself created Hanrahan
And drove him drunk or sober through the dawn
From somewhere in the neighbouring cottages.

Caught by an old man's juggleries
He stumbled, tumbled, fumbled to and fro
And had but broken knees for hire
And horrible splendour of desire;
I thought it all out twenty years ago:

Good fellows shuffled cards in an old bawn;
And when that ancient ruffian's turn was on
He so bewitched the cards under his thumb
That all but the one card became
A pack of hounds and not a pack of cards,
And that he changed into a hare.
Hanrahan rose in frenzy there
And followed up those baying creatures towards -

O towards I have forgotten what - enough!
I must recall a man that neither love
Nor music nor an enemy's clipped ear
Could, he was so harried, cheer;
A figure that has grown so fabulous
There's not a neighbour left to say
When he finished his dog's day:
An ancient bankrupt master of this house.

Before that ruin came, for centuries,
Rough men-at-arms, cross-gartered to the knees

Or shod in iron, climbed the narrow stairs,
And certain men-at-arms there were
Whose images, in the Great Memory stored,
Come with loud cry and panting breast
To break upon a sleeper's rest
While their great wooden dice beat on the board.

As I would question all, come all who can;
Come old, necessitous. half-mounted man;
And bring beauty's blind rambling celebrant;
The red man the juggler sent
Through God-forsaken meadows; Mrs. French,
Gifted with so fine an ear;
The man drowned in a bog's mire,
When mocking Muses chose the country wench.

Did all old men and women, rich and poor,
Who trod upon these rocks or passed this door,
Whether in public or in secret rage
As I do now against old age?
But I have found an answer in those eyes
That are impatient to be gone;
Go therefore; but leave Hanrahan,
For I need all his mighty memories.

Old lecher with a love on every wind,
Bring up out of that deep considering mind
All that you have discovered in the grave,
For it is certain that you have
Reckoned up every unforeknown, unseeing
plunge, lured by a softening eye,
Or by a touch or a sigh,
Into the labyrinth of another's being;

Does the imagination dwell the most
Upon a woman won or woman lost?
If on the lost, admit you turned aside
From a great labyrinth out of pride,
Cowardice, some silly over-subtle thought
Or anything called conscience once;
And that if memory recur, the sun's
Under eclipse and the day blotted out.

III

It is time that I wrote my will;
I choose upstanding men
That climb the streams until
The fountain leap, and at dawn
Drop their cast at the side
Of dripping stone; I declare

They shall inherit my pride,
The pride of people that were
Bound neither to Cause nor to State.
Neither to slaves that were spat on,
Nor to the tyrants that spat,
The people of Burke and of Grattan
That gave, though free to refuse -
pride, like that of the morn,
When the headlong light is loose,
Or that of the fabulous horn,
Or that of the sudden shower
When all streams are dry,
Or that of the hour
When the swan must fix his eye
Upon a fading gleam,
Float out upon a long
Last reach of glittering stream
And there sing his last song.
And I declare my faith:
I mock plotinus' thought
And cry in plato's teeth,
Death and life were not
Till man made up the whole,
Made lock, stock and barrel
Out of his bitter soul,
Aye, sun and moon and star, all,

And further add to that
That, being dead, we rise,
Dream and so create
Translunar paradise.
I have prepared my peace
With learned Italian things
And the proud stones of Greece,
Poet's imaginings
And memories of love,
Memories of the words of women,
All those things whereof
Man makes a superhuman,
Mirror-resembling dream.

As at the loophole there
The daws chatter and scream,
And drop twigs layer upon layer.
When they have mounted up,
The mother bird will rest
On their hollow top,
And so warm her wild nest.

I leave both faith and pride
To young upstanding men
Climbing the mountain-side,

That under bursting dawn
They may drop a fly;
Being of that metal made
Till it was broken by
This sedentary trade.

Now shall I make my soul,
Compelling it to study
In a learned school
Till the wreck of body,
Slow decay of blood,
Testy delirium
Or dull decrepitude,
Or what worse evil come -
The death of friends, or death
Of every brilliant eye
That made a catch in the breath -
Seem but the clouds of the sky
When the horizon fades;
Or a bird's sleepy cry
Among the deepening shades.

SEPTEMBER 1913

What need you, being come to sense,
But fumble in a greasy till
And add the halfpence to the pence
And prayer to shivering prayer, until
You have dried the marrow from the bone?
For men were born to pray and save:
Romantic Ireland's dead and gone,
It's with O'Leary in the grave.

Yet they were of a different kind,
The names that stilled your childish play,
They have gone about the world like wind,
But little time had they to pray
For whom the hangman's rope was spun,
And what, God help us, could they save?
Romantic Ireland's dead and gone,
It's with O'Leary in the grave.

Was it for this the wild geese spread
The grey wing upon every tide;
For this that all that blood was shed,
For this Edward Fitzgerald died,
And Robert Emmet and Wolfe Tone,
All that delirium of the brave?
Romantic Ireland's dead and gone,
It's with O'Leary in the grave.

Yet could we turn the years again,
And call those exiles as they were
In all their loneliness and pain,
You'd cry, 'Some woman's yellow hair
Has maddened every mother's son':
They weighed so lightly what they gave.
But let them be, they're dead and gone,
They're with O'Leary in the grave.

HE WISHES FOR THE CLOTHS OF HEAVEN

Had I the heavens' embroidered cloths,
Enwrought with golden and silver light

The blue and the dim and the dark cloths
Of night and light and the half-light,
I would spread the cloths under your feet:
But I, being poor, have only my dreams;
I have spread my dreams under your feet;
Tread softly because you tread on my dreams.

A SONG FROM 'THE PLAYER QUEEN'

My mother dandled me and sang,
'How young it is, how young!'
And made a golden cradle
That on a willow swung.

'He went away,' my mother sang,
'When I was brought to bed,'
And all the while her needle pulled
The gold and silver thread.

She pulled the thread and bit the thread
And made a golden gown,
And wept because she had dreamt that I
Was born to wear a crown.

'When she was got,' my mother sang,
I heard a sea-mew cry,
And saw a flake of the yellow foam
That dropped upon my thigh.'

How therefore could she help but braid
The gold into my hair,
And dream that I should carry
The golden top of care?

The Second Coming by William Butler Yeats
Turning and turning in the widening gyre
The falcon cannot hear the falconer;
Things fall apart; the centre cannot hold;
Mere anarchy is loosed upon the world,
The blood-dimmed tide is loosed, and everywhere
The ceremony of innocence is drowned;
The best lack all conviction, while the worst
Are full of passionate intensity.

Surely some revelation is at hand;
Surely the Second Coming is at hand.
The Second Coming! Hardly are those words out
When a vast image out of Spiritus Mundi

Troubles my sight: somewhere in sands of the desert
A shape with lion body and the head of a man,
A gaze blank and pitiless as the sun,
Is moving its slow thighs, while all about it
Reel shadows of the indignant desert birds.
The darkness drops again; but now I know
That twenty centuries of stony sleep
Were vexed to nightmare by a rocking cradle,
And what rough beast, its hour come round at last,
Slouches towards Bethlehem to be born?

An Irish Airman Forsees His Death
I know that I shall meet my fate
Somewhere among the clouds above;
Those that I fight I do not hate,
Those that I guard I do not love;
My county is Kiltartan Cross,
My countrymen Kiltartan's poor,
No likely end could bring them loss
Or leave them happier than before.
Nor law, nor duty bade me fight,
Nor public men, nor cheering crowds,
A lonely impulse of delight
Drove to this tumult in the clouds;
I balanced all, brought all to mind,

The years to come seemed waste of breath,
A waste of breath the years behind
In balance with this life, this death.

THE STOLEN CHILD

Where dips the rocky highland
Of Sleuth Wood in the lake,
There lies a leafy island
Where flapping herons wake
The drowsy water-rats;
There we've hid our faery vats,
Full of berries
And of reddest stolen cherries.
Come away, O human child!
To the waters and the wild
With a faery, hand in hand,
For the world's more full of weeping than you can understand.

Where the wave of moonlight glosses
The dim grey sands with light,
Far off by furthest Rosses

We foot it all the night,
Weaving olden dances,
Mingling hands and mingling glances
Till the moon has taken flight;
To and fro we leap
And chase the frothy bubbles,
While the world is full of troubles
And is anxious in its sleep.
Come away, O human child!
To the waters and the wild
With a faery, hand in hand,
For the world's more full of weeping than you
can understand.

Where the wandering water gushes
From the hills above Glen-Car,.
In pools among the rushes
That scarce could bathe a star,
We seek for slumbering trout
And whispering in their ears
Give them unquiet dreams;
Leaning softly out
From ferns that drop their tears
Over the young streams.
Come away, O human child!
To to waters and the wild

With a faery, hand in hand,
For to world's more full of weeping than you
can understand.

Away with us he's going,
The solemn-eyed:
He'll hear no more the lowing
Of the calves on the warm hillside
Or the kettle on the hob
Sing peace into his breast,
Or see the brown mice bob
Round and round the oatmeal-chest.
For be comes, the human child,
To the waters and the wild
With a faery, hand in hand,
from a world more full of weeping than you.

❖ ❖ ❖

A PRAYER FOR MY DAUGHTER

Once more the storm is howling, and half hid
Under this cradle-hood and coverlid
My child sleeps on. There is no obstacle
But Gregory's wood and one bare hill

Whereby the haystack- and roof-levelling wind.
Bred on the Atlantic, can be stayed;
And for an hour I have walked and prayed
Because of the great gloom that is in my mind.

I have walked and prayed for this young child an hour
And heard the sea-wind scream upon the tower,
And-under the arches of the bridge, and scream
In the elms above the flooded stream;
Imagining in excited reverie
That the future years had come,
Dancing to a frenzied drum,
Out of the murderous innocence of the sea.

May she be granted beauty and yet not
Beauty to make a stranger's eye distraught,
Or hers before a looking-glass, for such,
Being made beautiful overmuch,
Consider beauty a sufficient end,
Lose natural kindness and maybe
The heart-revealing intimacy
That chooses right, and never find a friend.

Helen being chosen found life flat and dull
And later had much trouble from a fool,

While that great Queen, that rose out of the spray,
Being fatherless could have her way
Yet chose a bandy-leggèd smith for man.
It's certain that fine women eat
A crazy salad with their meat
Whereby the Horn of plenty is undone.

In courtesy I'd have her chiefly learned;
Hearts are not had as a gift but hearts are earned
By those that are not entirely beautiful;
Yet many, that have played the fool
For beauty's very self, has charm made wisc.
And many a poor man that has roved,
Loved and thought himself beloved,
From a glad kindness cannot take his eyes.

May she become a flourishing hidden tree
That all her thoughts may like the linnet be,
And have no business but dispensing round
Their magnanimities of sound,
Nor but in merriment begin a chase,
Nor but in merriment a quarrel.
O may she live like some green laurel
Rooted in one dear perpetual place.

My mind, because the minds that I have loved,
The sort of beauty that I have approved,
Prosper but little, has dried up of late,
Yet knows that to be choked with hate
May well be of all evil chances chief.
If there's no hatred in a mind
Assault and battery of the wind
Can never tear the linnet from the leaf.

An intellectual hatred is the worst,
So let her think opinions are accursed.
Have I not seen the loveliest woman born
Out of the mouth of plenty's horn,
Because of her opinionated mind
Barter that horn and every good
By quiet natures understood
For an old bellows full of angry wind?

Considering that, all hatred driven hence,
The soul recovers radical innocence
And learns at last that it is self-delighting,
Self-appeasing, self-affrighting,
And that its own sweet will is Heaven's will;
She can, though every face should scowl
And every windy quarter howl
Or every bellows burst, be happy Still.

And may her bridegroom bring her to a house
Where all's accustomed, ceremonious;
For arrogance and hatred are the wares
Peddled in the thoroughfares.
How but in custom and in ceremony
Are innocence and beauty born?
Ceremony's a name for the rich horn,
And custom for the spreading laurel tree.

WHEN YOU ARE OLD

When you are old and grey and full of sleep,
And nodding by the fire, take down this book,
And slowly read, and dream of the soft look
Your eyes had once, and of their shadows deep;

How many loved your moments of glad grace,
And loved your beauty with love false or true,
But one man loved the pilgrim Soul in you,
And loved the sorrows of your changing face;

And bending down beside the glowing bars,
Murmur, a little sadly, how Love fled
And paced upon the mountains overhead
And hid his face amid a crowd of stars.

LEDA AND THE SWAN

A sudden blow: the great wings beating still
Above the staggering girl, her thighs caressed
By the dark webs, her nape caught in his bill,
He holds her helpless breast upon his breast.

How can those terrified vague fingers push
The feathered glory from her loosening thighs?
And how can body, laid in that white rush,
But feel the strange heart beating where it lies?

A shudder in the loins engenders there
The broken wall, the burning roof and tower
And Agamemnon dead.
Being so caught up,
So mastered by the brute blood of the air,

Did she put on his knowledge with his power
Before the indifferent beak could let her drop?

THE FISHERMAN

Although I can see him still.
The freckled man who goes
To a grey place on a hill
In grey Connemara clothes
At dawn to cast his flies,
It's long since I began
To call up to the eyes
This wise and simple man.
All day I'd looked in the face
What I had hoped 'twould be
To write for my own race
And the reality;
The living men that I hate,
The dead man that I loved,
The craven man in his seat,
The insolent unreproved,
And no knave brought to book
Who has won a drunken cheer,

The witty man and his joke
Aimed at the commonest ear,
The clever man who cries
The catch-cries of the clown,
The beating down of the wise
And great Art beaten down.

Maybe a twelvemonth since
Suddenly I began,
In scorn of this audience,
Imagining a man,
And his sun-freckled face,
And grey Connemara cloth,
Climbing up to a place
Where stone is dark under froth,
And the down-turn of his wrist
When the flies drop in the stream;
A man who does not exist,
A man who is but a dream;
And cried, 'Before I am old
I shall have written him one
poem maybe as cold
And passionate as the dawn.'

DEATH

Nor dread nor hope attend
A dying animal;
A man awaits his end
Dreading and hoping all;
Many times he died,
Many times rose again.
A great man in his pride
Confronting murderous men
Casts derision upon
Supersession of breath;
He knows death to the bone -
Man has created death.

❖ ❖ ❖

AMONG SCHOOL CHILDREN

I

I walk through the long schoolroom questioning;
A kind old nun in a white hood replies;

The children learn to cipher and to sing,
To study reading-books and histories,
To cut and sew, be neat in everything
In the best modern way - the children's eyes
In momentary wonder stare upon
A sixty-year-old smiling public man.

II

I dream of a Ledaean body, bent
Above a sinking fire. a tale that she
Told of a harsh reproof, or trivial event
That changed some childish day to tragedy -
Told, and it seemed that our two natures blent
Into a sphere from youthful sympathy,
Or else, to alter Plato's parable,
Into the yolk and white of the one shell.

III

And thinking of that fit of grief or rage
I look upon one child or t'other there
And wonder if she stood so at that age -
For even daughters of the swan can share
Something of every paddler's heritage -
And had that colour upon cheek or hair,
And thereupon my heart is driven wild:

She stands before me as a living child.

IV

Her present image floats into the mind -
Did Quattrocento finger fashion it
Hollow of cheek as though it drank the wind
And took a mess of shadows for its meat?
And I though never of Ledaean kind
Had pretty plumage once - enough of that,
Better to smile on all that smile, and show
There is a comfortable kind of old scarecrow.

V

What youthful mother, a shape upon her lap
Honey of generation had betrayed,
And that must sleep, shriek, struggle to escape
As recollection or the drug decide,
Would think her Son, did she but see that shape
With sixty or more winters on its head,
A compensation for the pang of his birth,
Or the uncertainty of his setting forth?

VI

Plato thought nature but a spume that plays
Upon a ghostly paradigm of things;

Solider Aristotle played the taws
Upon the bottom of a king of kings;
World-famous golden-thighed Pythagoras
Fingered upon a fiddle-stick or strings
What a star sang and careless Muses heard:
Old clothes upon old sticks to scare a bird.

VII

Both nuns and mothers worship images,
But thos the candles light are not as those
That animate a mother's reveries,
But keep a marble or a bronze repose.
And yet they too break hearts - O presences
That passion, piety or affection knows,
And that all heavenly glory symbolise -
O self-born mockers of man's enterprise;

VIII

Labour is blossoming or dancing where
The body is not bruised to pleasure soul.
Nor beauty born out of its own despair,
Nor blear-eyed wisdom out of midnight oil.
O chestnut-tree, great-rooted blossomer,
Are you the leaf, the blossom or the bole?

O body swayed to music, O brightening glance,
How can we know the dancer from the dance?

❖ ❖ ❖

EASTER, 1916

I have met them at close of day
Coming with vivid faces
From counter or desk among grey
Eighteenth-century houses.
I have passed with a nod of the head
Or polite meaningless words,
Or have lingered awhile and said
Polite meaningless words,
And thought before I had done
Of a mocking tale or a gibe
To please a companion
Around the fire at the club,
Being certain that they and I
But lived where motley is worn:
All changed, changed utterly:
A terrible beauty is born.

That woman's days were spent

In ignorant good-will,
Her nights in argument
Until her voice grew shrill.
What voice more sweet than hers
When, young and beautiful,
She rode to harriers?
This man had kept a school
And rode our winged horse;
This other his helper and friend
Was coming into his force;
He might have won fame in the end,
So sensitive his nature seemed,
So daring and sweet his thought.
This other man I had dreamed
A drunken, vainglorious lout.
He had done most bitter wrong
To some who are near my heart,
Yet I number him in the song;
He, too, has resigned his part
In the casual comedy;
He, too, has been changed in his turn,
Transformed utterly:
A terrible beauty is born.

Hearts with one purpose alone
Through summer and winter seem

Enchanted to a stone
To trouble the living stream.
The horse that comes from the road.
The rider, the birds that range
From cloud to tumbling cloud,
Minute by minute they change;
A shadow of cloud on the stream
Changes minute by minute;
A horse-hoof slides on the brim,
And a horse plashes within it;
The long-legged moor-hens dive,
And hens to moor-cocks call;
Minute by minute they live:
The stone's in the midst of all.

Too long a sacrifice
Can make a stone of the heart.
O when may it suffice?
That is Heaven's part, our part
To murmur name upon name,
As a mother names her child
When sleep at last has come
On limbs that had run wild.
What is it but nightfall?
No, no, not night but death;

Was it needless death after all?
For England may keep faith
For all that is done and said.
We know their dream; enough
To know they dreamed and are dead;
And what if excess of love
Bewildered them till they died?
I write it out in a verse -
MacDonagh and MacBride
And Connolly and pearse
Now and in time to be,
Wherever green is worn,
Are changed, changed utterly:
A terrible beauty is born.

THE SORROW OF LOVE

The brawling of a sparrow in the eaves,
The brilliant moon and all the milky sky,
And all that famous harmony of leaves,
Had blotted out man's image and his cry.

A girl arose that had red mournful lips
And seemed the greatness of the world in tears,
Doomed like Odysseus and the labouring ships
And proud as Priam murdered with his peers;

Arose, and on the instant clamorous eaves,
A climbing moon upon an empty sky,
And all that lamentation of the leaves,
Could but compose man's image and his cry.

LOVE'S LONELINESS

Old fathers, great-grandfathers,
Rise as kindred should.
If ever lover's loneliness
Came where you stood,
Pray that Heaven protect us
That protect your blood.

The mountain throws a shadow,
Thin is the moon's horn;
What did we remember
Under the ragged thorn?

Dread has followed longing,
And our hearts are torn.

AN ACRE OF GRASS

Picture and book remain,
An acre of green grass
For air and exercise,
Now strength of body goes;
Midnight, an old house
Where nothing stirs but a mouse.

My temptation is quiet.
Here at life's end
Neither loose imagination,
Nor the mill of the mind
Consuming its rag and bonc,
Can make the truth known.

Grant me an old man's frenzy,
Myself must I remake
Till I am Timon and Lear
Or that William Blake

Who beat upon the wall
Till Truth obeyed his call;

A mind Michael Angelo knew
That can pierce the clouds,
Or inspired by frenzy
Shake the dead in their shrouds;
Forgotten else by mankind,
An old man's eagle mind.

A PRAYER FOR OLD AGE

God guard me from those thoughts men think
In the mind alone;
He that sings a lasting song
Thinks in a marrow-bone;

From all that makes a wise old man
That can be praised of all;
O what am I that I should not seem
For the song's sake a fool?

I pray -- for word is out

And prayer comes round again --
That I may seem, though I die old,
A foolish, passionate man.

A LAST CONFESSION

What lively lad most pleasured me
Of all that with me lay?
I answer that I gave my soul
And loved in misery,
But had great pleasure with a lad
That I loved bodily.

Flinging from his arms I laughed
To think his passion such
He fancied that I gave a soul
Did but our bodies touch,
And laughed upon his breast to think
Beast gave beast as much.

I gave what other women gave
That stepped out of their clothes.
But when this soul, its body off,

Naked to naked goes,
He it has found shall find therein
What none other knows,

And give his own and take his own
And rule in his own right;
And though it loved in misery
Close and cling so tight,
There's not a bird of day that dare
Extinguish that delight.

VACILLATION

I

Between extremities
Man runs his course;
A brand, or flaming breath.
Comes to destroy
All those antinomies
Of day and night;
The body calls it death,
The heart remorse.

But if these be right
What is joy?

II

A tree there is that from its topmost bough
Is half all glittering flame and half all green
Abounding foliage moistened with the dew;
And half is half and yet is all the scene;
And half and half consume what they renew,
And he that Attis' image hangs between
That staring fury and the blind lush leaf
May know not what he knows, but knows not grief

III

Get all the gold and silver that you can,
Satisfy ambition, animate
The trivial days and ram them with the sun,
And yet upon these maxims meditate:
All women dote upon an idle man
Although their children need a rich estate;
No man has ever lived that had enough
Of children's gratitude or woman's love.

No longer in Lethean foliage caught
Begin the preparation for your death
And from the fortieth winter by that thought
Test every work of intellect or faith,
And everything that your own hands have wrought
And call those works extravagance of breath
That are not suited for such men as come
proud, open-eyed and laughing to the tomb.

IV

My fiftieth year had come and gone,
I sat, a solitary man,
In a crowded London shop,
An open book and empty cup
On the marble table-top.
While on the shop and street I gazed
My body of a sudden blazed;
And twenty minutes more or less
It seemed, so great my happiness,
That I was blessed and could bless.

V

Although the summer Sunlight gild
Cloudy leafage of the sky,

Or wintry moonlight sink the field
In storm-scattered intricacy,
I cannot look thereon,
Responsibility so weighs me down.

Things said or done long years ago,
Or things I did not do or say
But thought that I might say or do,
Weigh me down, and not a day
But something is recalled,
My conscience or my vanity appalled.

VI

A rivery field spread out below,
An odour of the new-mown hay
In his nostrils, the great lord of Chou
Cried, casting off the mountain snow,
`Let all things pass away.'

Wheels by milk-white asses drawn
Where Babylon or Nineveh
Rose; some conquer drew rein
And cried to battle-weary men,
Let all things pass away.'

From man's blood-sodden heart are sprung
Those branches of the night and day
Where the gaudy moon is hung.
What's the meaning of all song?
`Let all things pass away.'

VII

The Soul. Seek out reality, leave things that seem.
The Heart. What, be a singer born and lack a theme?
The Soul. Isaiah's coal, what more can man desire?
The Heart. Struck dumb in the simplicity of fire!
The Soul. Look on that fire, salvation walks within.
The Heart. What theme had Homer but original sin?

VIII

Must we part, Von Hugel, though much alike, for we
Accept the miracles of the saints and honour sanctity?
The body of Saint Teresa lies undecayed in tomb,
Bathed in miraculous oil, sweet odours from it come,
Healing from its lettered slab. Those self-same hands perchance
Eternalised the body of a modern saint that once

Had scooped out pharaoh's mummy. I - though heart might find relief
Did I become a Christian man and choose for my belief
What seems most welcome in the tomb - play a pre-destined part.
Homer is my example and his unchristened heart.
The lion and the honeycomb, what has Scripture said?
So get you gone, Von Hugel, though with blessings on your head.

THE LADY'S SECOND SONG

What sort of man is coming
To lie between your feet?
What matter, we are but women.
Wash; make your body sweet;
I have cupboards of dried fragrance.
I can strew the sheet.
The Lord have mercy upon us.

He shall love my soul as though
Body were not at all,
He shall love your body
Untroubled by the soul,

Love cram love's two divisions
Yet keep his substance whole.
The Lord have mercy upon us.

Soul must learn a love that is
proper to my breast,
Limbs a Love in common
With every noble beast.
If soul may look and body touch,
Which is the more blest?
The Lord have mercy upon us.

NINETEEN HUNDRED AND NINETEEN

I

Many ingenious lovely things are gone
That seemed sheer miracle to the multitude,
protected from the circle of the moon
That pitches common things about. There stood
Amid the ornamental bronze and stone
An ancient image made of olive wood -
And gone are phidias' famous ivories

And all the golden grasshoppers and bees.

We too had many pretty toys when young:
A law indifferent to blame or praise,
To bribe or threat; habits that made old wrong
Melt down, as it were wax in the sun's rays;
Public opinion ripening for so long
We thought it would outlive all future days.
O what fine thought we had because we thought
That the worst rogues and rascals had died out.

All teeth were drawn, all ancient tricks unlearned,
And a great army but a showy thing;
What matter that no cannon had been turned
Into a ploughshare? Parliament and king
Thought that unless a little powder burned
The trumpeters might burst with trumpeting
And yet it lack all glory; and perchance
The guardsmen's drowsy chargers would not prance.

Now days are dragon-ridden, the nightmare
Rides upon sleep: a drunken soldiery
Can leave the mother, murdered at her door,
To crawl in her own blood, and go scot-free;
The night can sweat with terror as before

We pieced our thoughts into philosophy,
And planned to bring the world under a rule,
Who are but weasels fighting in a hole.

He who can read the signs nor sink unmanned
Into the half-deceit of some intoxicant
From shallow wits; who knows no work can stand,
Whether health, wealth or peace of mind were spent
On master-work of intellect or hand,
No honour leave its mighty monument,
Has but one comfort left: all triumph would
But break upon his ghostly solitude.
But is there any comfort to be found?

Man is in love and loves what vanishes,
What more is there to say? That country round
None dared admit, if Such a thought were his,
Incendiary or bigot could be found
To burn that stump on the Acropolis,
Or break in bits the famous ivories
Or traffic in the grasshoppers or bees.

THE LIVING BEAUTY

I bade, because the wick and oil are spent
And frozen are the channels of the blood,
My discontented heart to draw content
From beauty that is cast out of a mould
In bronze, or that in dazzling marble appears,
Appears, but when wc have gone is gone again,
Being more indifferent to our solitude
Than 'twere an apparition. O heart, we are old;
The living beauty is for younger men:
We cannot pay its rribute of wild tears.

THE ROSE TREE

'O words are lightly spoken,'
Said Pearse to Connolly,
'Maybe a breath of politic words
Has withered our Rose Tree;

Or maybe but a wind that blows
Across the bitter sea.'

'It needs to be but watered,'
James Connolly replied,
'To make the green come out again
And spread on every side,
And shake the blossom from the bud
To be the garden's pride.'

'But where can we draw water,'
Said Pearse to Connolly,
'When all the wells are parched away?
O plain as plain can be
There's nothing but our own red blood
Can make a right Rose Tree.'

THE SONG OF THE OLD MOTHER

I rise in the dawn, and I kneel and blow
Till the seed of the fire flicker and glow;
And then I must scrub and bake and sweep
Till stars are beginning to blink and peep;

And the young lie long and dream in their bed
Of the matching of ribbons for bosom and head,
And their day goes over in idleness,
And they sigh if the wind but lift a tress:
While I must work because I am old,
And the seed of the fire gets feeble and cold.

LAPIS LAZULI

(For Harry Clifton)

I HAVE heard that hysterical women say
They are sick of the palette and fiddle-bow.
Of poets that are always gay,
For everybody knows or else should know
That if nothing drastic is done
Aeroplane and Zeppelin will come out.
Pitch like King Billy bomb-balls in
Until the town lie beaten flat.

All perform their tragic play,
There struts Hamlet, there is Lear,
That's Ophelia, that Cordelia;

Yet they, should the last scene be there,
The great stage curtain about to drop,
If worthy their prominent part in the play,
Do not break up their lines to weep.
They know that Hamlet and Lear are gay;
Gaiety transfiguring all that dread.
All men have aimed at, found and lost;
Black out; Heaven blazing into the head:
Tragedy wrought to its uttermost.
Though Hamlet rambles and Lear rages,
And all the drop-scenes drop at once
Upon a hundred thousand stages,
It cannot grow by an inch or an ounce.

On their own feet they came, or On shipboard,'
Camel-back; horse-back, ass-back, mule-back,
Old civilisations put to the sword.
Then they and their wisdom went to rack:
No handiwork of Callimachus,
Who handled marble as if it were bronze,
Made draperies that seemed to rise
When sea-wind swept the corner, stands;
His long lamp-chimney shaped like the stem
Of a slender palm, stood but a day;
All things fall and are built again,

And those that build them again are gay.

Two Chinamen, behind them a third,
Are carved in lapis lazuli,
Over them flies a long-legged bird,
A symbol of longevity;
The third, doubtless a serving-man,
Carries a musical instmmment.

Every discoloration of the stone,
Every accidental crack or dent,
Seems a water-course or an avalanche,
Or lofty slope where it still snows
Though doubtless plum or cherry-branch
Sweetens the little half-way house
Those Chinamen climb towards, and I
Delight to imagine them seated there;
There, on the mountain and the sky,
On all the tragic scene they stare.
One asks for mournful melodies;
Accomplished fingers begin to play.
Their eyes mid many wrinkles, their eyes,
Their ancient, glittering eyes, are gay.

A DRUNKEN MAN'S PRAISE OF SOBRIETY

Come swish around, my pretty punk,
And keep me dancing still
That I may stay a sober man
Although I drink my fill.
Sobriety is a jewel
That I do much adore;
And therefore keep me dancing
Though drunkards lie and snore.
O mind your feet, O mind your feet,
Keep dancing like a wave,
And under every dancer
A dead man in his grave.
No ups and downs, my pretty,
A mermaid, not a punk;
A drunkard is a dead man,
And all dead men are drunk.

THE SONG OF WANDERING AENGUS

I went out to the hazel wood,
Because a fire was in my head,
And cut and peeled a hazel wand,
And hooked a berry to a thread;
And when white moths were on the wing,
And moth-like stars were flickering out,
I dropped the berry in a stream
And caught a little silver trout.
When I had laid it on the floor
I went to blow the fire aflame,
But something rustled on the floor,
And some one called me by my name:
It had become a glimmering girl
With apple blossom in her hair
Who called me by my name and ran
And faded through the brightening air.
Though I am old with wandering
Through hollow lads and hilly lands.
I will find out where she has gone,
And kiss her lips and take her hands;

And walk among long dappled grass,
And pluck till time and times are done
The silver apples of the moon,
The golden apples of the sun.

THE CHOICE

The intellect of man is forced to choose
perfection of the life, or of the work,
And if it take the second must refuse
A heavenly mansion, raging in the dark.
When all that story's finished, what's the news?
In luck or out the toil has left its mark:
That old perplexity an empty purse,
Or the day's vanity, the night's remorse.

THE FALLING OF THE LEAVES

Autumn is over the long leaves that love us,
And over the mice in the barley sheaves;
Yellow the leaves of the rowan above us,

And yellow the wet wild-strawberry leaves.

The hour of the waning of love has beset us,
And weary and worn are our sad souls now;
Let us patt, ere the season of passion forget us,
With a kiss and a tear on thy drooping brow.

A CRAZED GIRL

That crazed girl improvising her music.
Her poetry, dancing upon the shore,
Her soul in division from itself
Climbing, falling She knew not where,
Hiding amid the cargo of a steamship,
Her knee-cap broken, that girl I declare
A beautiful lofty thing, or a thing
Heroically lost, heroically found.

No matter what disaster occurred
She stood in desperate music wound,
Wound, wound, and she made in her triumph
Where the bales and the baskets lay

No common intelligible sound
But sang, 'O sea-starved, hungry sea.'

BROKEN DREAMS

There is grey in your hair.
Young men no longer suddenly catch their breath
When you are passing;
But maybe some old gaffer mutters a blessing
Because it was your prayer
Recovered him upon the bed of death.
For your sole sake - that all heart's ache have known,
And given to others all heart's ache,
From meagre girlhood's putting on
Burdensome beauty -- for your sole sake
Heaven has put away the stroke of her doom,
So great her portion in that peace you make
By merely walking in a room.

Your beauty can but leave among us
Vague memories, nothing but memories.
A young man when the old men are done talking
Will say to an old man, 'Tell me of that lady

The poet stubborn with his passion sang us
When age might well have chilled his blood.'

Vague memories, nothing but memories,
But in the grave all, all, shall be renewed.
The certainty that I shall see that lady
Leaning or standing or walking
In the first loveliness of womanhood,
And with the fervour of my youthful eyes,
Has set me muttering like a fool.

You are more beautiful than any one,
And yet your body had a flaw:
Your small hands were not beautiful,
And I am afraid that you will run
And paddle to the wrist
In that mysterious, always brimming lake
Where those What have obeyed the holy law
paddle and are perfect. Leave unchanged
The hands that I have kissed,
For old sake's sake.

The last stroke of midnight dies.
All day in the one chair
From dream to dream and rhyme to rhyme I have ranged

In rambling talk with an image of air:
Vague memories, nothing but memories.

A DIALOGUE OF SELF AND SOUL

My Soul. I summon to the winding ancient stair;
Set all your mind upon the steep ascent,
Upon the broken, crumbling battlement,
Upon the breathless starlit air,
"Upon the star that marks the hidden pole;
Fix every wandering thought upon
That quarter where all thought is done:
Who can distinguish darkness from the soul

My Self. The consecretes blade upon my knees
Is Sato's ancient blade, still as it was,
Still razor-keen, still like a looking-glass
Unspotted by the centuries;
That flowering, silken, old embroidery, torn
From some court-lady's dress and round
The wodden scabbard bound and wound
Can, tattered, still protect, faded adorn

My Soul. Why should the imagination of a man
Long past his prime remember things that are
Emblematical of love and war?
Think of ancestral night that can,
If but imagination scorn the earth
And interllect is wandering
To this and that and t'other thing,
Deliver from the crime of death and birth.

My Self. Montashigi, third of his family, fashioned it
Five hundred years ago, about it lie
Flowers from I know not what embroidery -
Heart's purple - and all these I set
For emblems of the day against the tower
Emblematical of the night,
And claim as by a soldier's right
A charter to commit the crime once more.

My Soul. Such fullness in that quarter overflows
And falls into the basin of the mind
That man is stricken deaf and dumb and blind,
For intellect no longer knows
Is from the Ought, or knower from the Known -
That is to say, ascends to Heaven;
Only the dead can be forgiven;

But when I think of that my tongue's a stone.

II

My Self. A living man is blind and drinks his drop.
What matter if the ditches are impure?
What matter if I live it all once more?
Endure that toil of growing up;
The ignominy of boyhood; the distress
Of boyhood changing into man;
The unfinished man and his pain
Brought face to face with his own clumsiness;

The finished man among his enemies? -
How in the name of Heaven can he escape
That defiling and disfigured shape
The mirror of malicious eyes
Casts upon his eyes until at last
He thinks that shape must be his shape?
And what's the good of an escape
If honour find him in the wintry blast?

I am content to live it all again
And yet again, if it be life to pitch
Into the frog-spawn of a blind man's ditch,

A blind man battering blind men;
Or into that most fecund ditch of all,
The folly that man does
Or must suffer, if he woos
A proud woman not kindred of his soul.

I am content to follow to its source
Every event in action or in thought;
Measure the lot; forgive myself the lot!
When such as I cast out remorse
So great a sweetness flows into the breast
We must laugh and we must sing,
We are blest by everything,
Everything we look upon is blest.

NO SECOND TROY

Why should I blame her that she filled my days
With misery, or that she would of late
Have taught to ignorant men most violent ways,
Or hurled the little streets upon the great.
Had they but courage equal to desire?
What could have made her peaceful with a mind

That nobleness made simple as a fire,
With beauty like a tightened bow, a kind
That is not natural in an age like this,
Being high and solitary and most stern?
Why, what could she have done, being what she is?
Was there another Troy for her to burn?

❖ ❖ ❖

THE CIRCUS ANIMALS' DESERTION

I

I sought a theme and sought for it in vain,
I sought it daily for six weeks or so.
Maybe at last, being but a broken man,
I must be satisfied with my heart, although
Winter and summer till old age began
My circus animals were all on show,
Those stilted boys, that burnished chariot,
Lion and woman and the Lord knows what.

II

What can I but enumerate old themes?
First that sea-rider Oisin led by the nose
Through three enchanted islands, allegorical dreams,

Vain gaiety, vain battle, vain repose,
Themes of the embittered heart, or so it seems,
That might adorn old songs or courtly shows;
But what cared I that set him on to ride,
I, starved for the bosom of his faery bride?

And then a counter-truth filled out its play,
'The Countess Cathleen' was the name I gave it;
She, pity-crazed, had given her soul away,
But masterful Heaven had intetvened to save it.
I thought my dear must her own soul destroy,
So did fanaticism and hate enslave it,
And this brought forth a dream and soon enough
This dream itself had all my thought and love.

And when the Fool and Blind Man stole the bread
Cuchulain fought the ungovernable sea;
Heart-mysteries there, and yet when all is said
It was the dream itself enchanted me:
Character isolated by a deed
To engross the present and dominate memory.
players and painted stage took all my love,
And not those things that they were emblems of.

III

Those masterful images because complete
Grew in pure mind, but out of what began?
A mound of refuse or the sweepings of a street,
Old kettles, old bottles, and a broken can,
Old iron, old bones, old rags, that raving slut
Who keeps the till. Now that my ladder's gone,
I must lie down where all the ladders start
In the foul rag-and-bone shop of the heart.

THE DOLLS

A doll in the doll-maker's house
Looks at the cradle and bawls:
'That is an insult to us.'
But the oldest of all the dolls,
Who had seen, being kept for show,
Generations of his sort,
Out-screams the whole shelf: 'Although
There's not a man can report
Evil of this place,
The man and the woman bring
Hither, to our disgrace,

A noisy and filthy thing.'
Hearing him groan and stretch
The doll-maker's wife is aware
Her husband has heard the wretch,
And crouched by the arm of his chair,
She murmurs into his ear,
Head upon shoulder leant:
'My dear, my dear, O dear,
It was an accident.'

THE TWO TREES

Beloved, gaze in thine own heart,
The holy tree is growing there;
From joy the holy branches start,
And all the trembling flowers they bear.
The changing colours of its fruit
Have dowered the stars with metry light;
The surety of its hidden root
Has planted quiet in the night;
The shaking of its leafy head
Has given the waves their melody,
And made my lips and music wed,

Murmuring a wizard song for thee.
There the Joves a circle go,
The flaming circle of our days,
Gyring, spiring to and fro
In those great ignorant leafy ways;
Remembering all that shaken hair
And how the winged sandals dart,
Thine eyes grow full of tender care:

Beloved, gaze in thine own heart,
Gaze no more in the bitter glass
The demons, with their subtle guile.
Lift up before us when they pass,
Or only gaze a little while;
For there a fatal image grows
That the stormy night receives,
Roots half hidden under snows,
Broken boughs and blackened leaves.
For ill things turn to barrenness
In the dim glass the demons hold,
The glass of outer weariness,
Made when God slept in times of old.
There, through the broken branches, go
The ravens of unresting thought;
Flying, crying, to and fro,

Cruel claw and hungry throat,
Or else they stand and sniff the wind,
And shake their ragged wings; alas!
Thy tender eyes grow all unkind:
Gaze no more in the bitter glass.

WISDOM

The true faith discovered was
When painted panel, statuary.
Glass-mosaic, window-glass,
Amended what was told awry
By some peasant gospeller;
Swept the Sawdust from the floor
Of that working-carpenter.
Miracle had its playtime where
In damask clothed and on a seat
Chryselephantine, cedar-boarded,
His majestic Mother sat
Stitching at a purple hoarded
That He might be nobly breeched
In starry towers of Babylon
Noah's freshet never reached.

King Abundance got Him on
Innocence; and Wisdom He.
That cognomen sounded best
Considering what wild infancy
Drove horror from His Mother's breast.

A PRAYER FOR MY SON

Bid a strong ghost stand at the head
That my Michael may sleep sound,
Nor cry, nor turn in the bed
Till his morning meal come round;
And may departing twilight keep
All dread afar till morning's back.
That his mother may not lack
Her fill of sleep.

Bid the ghost have sword in fist:
Some there are, for I avow
Such devilish things exist,
Who have planned his murder, for they know
Of some most haughty deed or thought
That waits upon his future days,

And would through hatred of the bays
Bring that to nought.

Though You can fashion everything
From nothing every day, and teach
The morning stars to sing,
You have lacked articulate speech
To tell Your simplest want, and known,
Wailing upon a woman's knee,
All of that worst ignominy
Of flesh and bone;

And when through all the town there ran
The servants of Your enemy,
A woman and a man,
Unless the Holy Writings lie,
Hurried through the smooth and rough
And through the fertile and waste,
protecting, till the danger past,
With human love.

RUNNING TO PARADISE

As I came over Windy Gap
They threw a halfpenny into my cap.
For I am running to paradise;
And all that I need do is to wish
And somebody puts his hand in the dish
To throw me a bit of salted fish:
And there the king is but as the beggar.

My brother Mourteen is worn out
With skelping his big brawling lout,
And I am running to paradise;
A poor life, do what he can,
And though he keep a dog and a gun,
A serving-maid and a serving-man:
And there the king is but as the beggar.

Poor men have grown to be rich men,
And rich men grown to be poor again,
And I am running to paradise;

And many a darling wit's grown dull
That tossed a bare heel when at school,
Now it has filled a old sock full:
And there the king is but as the beggar.

The wind is old and still at play
While I must hurry upon my way.
For I am running to paradise;
Yet never have I lit on a friend
To take my fancy like the wind
That nobody can buy or bind:
And there the king is but as the beggar.

THOSE DANCING DAYS ARE GONE

Come, let me sing into your ear;
Those dancing days are gone,
All that silk and satin gear;
Crouch upon a stone,
Wrapping that foul body up
In as foul a rag:
I carry the sun in a golden cup.
The moon in a silver bag.

Curse as you may I sing it through;
What matter if the knave
That the most could pleasure you,
The children that he gave,
Are somewhere sleeping like a top
Under a marble flag?
I carry the sun in a golden cup.
The moon in a silver bag.

I thought it out this very day.
Noon upon the clock,
A man may put pretence away
Who leans upon a stick,
May sing, and sing until he drop,
Whether to maid or hag:
I carry the sun in a golden cup,
The moon in a silver bag.

NEVER GIVE ALL THE HEART

Never give all the heart, for love
Will hardly seem worth thinking of

To passionate women if it seem
Certain, and they never dream
That it fades out from kiss to kiss;
For everything that's lovely is
But a brief, dreamy. Kind delight.
O never give the heart outright,
For they, for all smooth lips can say,
Have given their hearts up to the play.
And who could play it well enough
If deaf and dumb and blind with love?
He that made this knows all the cost,
For he gave all his heart and lost.

THE WANDERINGS OF OISIN: I

S. Patrick. You who are bent, and bald, and blind,
With a heavy heart and a wandering mind,
Have known three centuries, poets sing,
Of dalliance with a demon thing.

Oisin. Sad to remember, sick with years,
The swift innumerable spears,
The horsemen with their floating hair,

And bowls of barley, honey, and wine,
Those merry couples dancing in tune,
And the white body that lay by mine;
But the tale, though words be lighter than air.
Must live to be old like the wandering moon.

Caoilte, and Conan, and Finn were there,
When we followed a deer with our baying hounds.
With Bran, Sceolan, and Lomair,
And passing the Firbolgs' burial-motmds,
Came to the cairn-heaped grassy hill
Where passionate Maeve is stony-still;
And found On the dove-grey edge of the sea
A pearl-pale, high-born lady, who rode
On a horse with bridle of findrinny;
And like a sunset were her lips,
A stormy sunset on doomed ships;
A citron colour gloomed in her hair,

But down to her feet white vesture flowed,
And with the glimmering crimson glowed
Of many a figured embroidery;
And it was bound with a pearl-pale shell
That wavered like the summer streams,
As her soft bosom rose and fell.

S. Patrick. You are still wrecked among heathen dreams.

Oisin. 'Why do you wind no horn?' she said
'And every hero droop his head?
The hornless deer is not more sad
That many a peaceful moment had,
More sleek than any granary mouse,
In his own leafy forest house
Among the waving fields of fern:
The hunting of heroes should be glad.'

'O pleasant woman,' answered Finn,
'We think on Oscar's pencilled urn,
And on the heroes lying slain
On Gabhra's raven-covered plain;
But where are your noble kith and kin,
And from what country do you ride?'

'My father and my mother are
Aengus and Edain, my own name
Niamh, and my country far
Beyond the tumbling of this tide.'

'What dream came with you that you came
Through bitter tide on foam-wet feet?

Did your companion wander away
From where the birds of Aengus wing?'
Thereon did she look haughty and sweet:
'I have not yet, war-weary king,
Been spoken of with any man;
Yet now I choose, for these four feet
Ran through the foam and ran to this
That I might have your son to kiss.'

'Were there no better than my son
That you through all that foam should run?'

'I loved no man, though kings besought,
Until the Danaan poets brought
Rhyme that rhymed upon Oisin's name,
And now I am dizzy with the thought
Of all that wisdom and the fame
Of battles broken by his hands,
Of stories builded by his words
That are like coloured Asian birds
At evening in their rainless lands.'

O Patrick, by your brazen bell,
There was no limb of mine but fell
Into a desperate gulph of love!

'You only will I wed,' I cried,
'And I will make a thousand songs,
And set your name all names above,
And captives bound with leathern thongs
Shall kneel and praise you, one by one,
At evening in my western dun.'

'O Oisin, mount by me and ride
To shores by the wash of the tremulous tide,
Where men have heaped no burial-mounds,
And the days pass by like a wayward tune,
Where broken faith has never been known
And the blushes of first love never have flown;
And there I will give you a hundred hounds;
No mightier creatures bay at the moon;
And a hundred robes of murmuring silk,
And a hundred calves and a hundred sheep
Whose long wool whiter than sea-froth flows,
And a hundred spears and a hundred bows,
And oil and wine and honey and milk,
And always never-anxious sleep;
While a hundred youths, mighty of limb,
But knowing nor tumult nor hate nor strife,
And a hundred ladies, merry as birds,
Who when they dance to a fitful measure

Have a speed like the speed of the salmon herds,
Shall follow your horn and obey your whim,
And you shall know the Danaan leisure;
And Niamh be with you for a wife.'
Then she sighed gently, 'It grows late.
Music and love and sleep await,
Where I would be when the white moon climbs,
The red sun falls and the world grows dim.'

And then I mounted and she bound me
With her triumphing arms around me,
And whispering to herself enwound me;
He shook himself and neighed three times:
Caoilte, Conan, and Finn came near,
And wept, and raised their lamenting hands,
And bid me stay, with many a tear;
But we rode out from the human lands.
In what far kingdom do you go'
Ah Fenians, with the shield and bow?
Or are you phantoms white as snow,
Whose lips had life's most prosperous glow?
O you, with whom in sloping vallcys,
Or down the dewy forest alleys,
I chased at morn the flying deer,
With whom I hurled the hurrying spear,

And heard the foemen's bucklers rattle,
And broke the heaving ranks of battle!
And Bran, Sceolan, and Lomair,
Where are you with your long rough hair?
You go not where the red deer feeds,
Nor tear the foemen from their steeds.

S. Patrick. Boast not, nor mourn with drooping head
Companions long accurst and dead,
And hounds for centuries dust and air.

Oisin. We galloped over the glossy sea:
I know not if days passed or hours,
And Niamh sang continually
Danaan songs, and their dewy showers
Of pensive laughter, unhuman sound,
Lulled weariness, and softly round
My human sorrow her white arms wound.
We galloped; now a hornless deer
Passed by us, chased by a phantom hound
All pearly white, save one red ear;
And now a lady rode like the wind
With an apple of gold in her tossing hand;
And a beautiful young man followed behind
With quenchless gaze and fluttering hair.

'Were these two born in the Danaan land,
Or have they breathed the mortal air?'

'Vex them no longer,' Niamh said,
And sighing bowed her gentle head,
And sighing laid the pearly tip
Of one long finger on my lip.

But now the moon like a white rose shone
In the pale west, and the sun'S rim sank,
And clouds atrayed their rank on rank
About his fading crimson ball:
The floor of Almhuín's hosting hall
Was not more level than the sea,
As, full of loving fantasy,
And with low murmurs, we rode on,
Where many a trumpet-twisted shell
That in immortal silence sleeps
Dreaming of her own melting hues,
Her golds, her ambers, and her blues,
Pierced with soft light the shallowing deeps.
But now a wandering land breeze came
And a far sound of feathery quires;
It seemed to blow from the dying flame,
They seemed to sing in the smouldering fires.

The horse towards the music raced,
Neighing along the lifeless waste;
Like sooty fingers, many a tree
Rose ever out of the warm sea;
And they were trembling ceaselessly,
As though they all were beating time,
Upon the centre of the sun,
To that low laughing woodland rhyme.
And, now our wandering hours were done,
We cantered to the shore, and knew
The reason of the trembling trees:
Round every branch the song-birds flew,
Or clung thereon like swarming bees;
While round the shore a million stood
Like drops of frozen rainbow light,
And pondered in a soft vain mood
Upon their shadows in the tide,
And told the purple deeps their pride,
And murmured snatches of delight;
And on the shores were many boats
With bending sterns and bending bows,
And carven figures on their prows
Of bitterns, and fish-eating stoats,
And swans with their exultant throats:
And where the wood and waters meet

We tied the horse in a leafy clump,
And Niamh blew three merry notes
Out of a little silver trump;
And then an answering whispering flew
Over the bare and woody land,
A whisper of impetuous feet,
And ever nearer, nearer grew;
And from the woods rushed out a band
Of men and ladies, hand in hand,
And singing, singing all together;
Their brows were white as fragrant milk,
Their cloaks made out of yellow silk,
And trimmed with many a crimson feather;
And when they saw the cloak I wore
Was dim with mire of a mortal shore,
They fingered it and gazed on me
And laughed like murmurs of the sea;
But Niamh with a swift distress
Bid them away and hold their peace;
And when they heard her voice they ran
And knelt there, every girl and man,
And kissed, as they would never cease,
Her pearl-pale hand and the hem of her dress.
She bade them bring us to the hall
Where Aengus dreams, from sun to sun,

A Druid dream of the end of days
When the stars are to wane and the world be done.

They led us by long and shadowy ways
Where drops of dew in myriads fall,
And tangled creepers every hour
Blossom in some new crimson flower,
And once a sudden laughter sprang
From all their lips, and once they sang
Together, while the dark woods rang,
And made in all their distant parts,
With boom of bees in honey-marts,
A rumour of delighted hearts.
And once a lady by my side
Gave me a harp, and bid me sing,
And touch the laughing silver string;
But when I sang of human joy
A sorrow wrapped each merry face,
And, patrick! by your beard, they wept,
Until one came, a tearful boy;
'A sadder creature never stept
Than this strange human bard,' he cried;
And caught the silver harp away,
And, weeping over the white strings, hurled
It down in a leaf-hid, hollow place

That kept dim waters from the sky;
And each one said, with a long, long sigh,
'O saddest harp in all the world,
Sleep there till the moon and the stars die!'

And now, still sad, we came to where
A beautiful young man dreamed within
A house of wattles, clay, and skin;
One hand upheld his beardless chin,
And one a sceptre flashing out
Wild flames of red and gold and blue,
Like to a merry wandering rout
Of dancers leaping in the air;
And men and ladies knelt them there
And showed their eyes with teardrops dim,
And with low murmurs prayed to him,
And kissed the sceptre with red lips,
And touched it with their finger-tips.
He held that flashing sceptre up.
'Joy drowns the twilight in the dew,
And fills with stars night's purple cup,
And wakes the sluggard seeds of corn,
And stirs the young kid's budding horn,
And makes the infant ferns unwrap,
And for the peewit paints his cap,

And rolls along the unwieldy sun,
And makes the little planets run:
And if joy were not on the earth,
There were an end of change and birth,
And Earth and Heaven and Hell would die,
And in some gloomy barrow lie
Folded like a frozen fly;
Then mock at Death and Time with glances
And wavering arms and wandering dances.

'Men's hearts of old were drops of flame
That from the saffron morning came,
Or drops of silver joy that fell
Out of the moon's pale twisted shell;
But now hearts cry that hearts are slaves,
And toss and turn in narrow caves;
But here there is nor law nor rule,
Nor have hands held a weary tool;
And here there is nor Change nor Death,
But only kind and merry breath,
For joy is God and God is joy.'
With one long glance for girl and boy
And the pale blossom of the moon,
He fell into a Druid swoon.

And in a wild and sudden dance
We mocked at Time and Fate and Chance
And swept out of the wattled hall
And came to where the dewdrops fall
Among the foamdrops of the sea,
And there we hushed the revelry;
And, gathering on our brows a frown,
Bent all our swaying bodies down,
And to the waves that glimmer by
That sloping green De Danaan sod
Sang, 'God is joy and joy is God,
And things that have grown sad are wicked,
And things that fear the dawn of the morrow
Or the grey wandering osprey Sorrow.'

We danced to where in the winding thicket
The damask roses, bloom on bloom,
Like crimson meteors hang in the gloom.
And bending over them softly said,
Bending over them in the dance,
With a swift and friendly glance
From dewy eyes: 'Upon the dead
Fall the leaves of other roses,
On the dead dim earth encloses:
But never, never on our graves,

Heaped beside the glimmering waves,
Shall fall the leaves of damask roses.
For neither Death nor Change comes near us,
And all listless hours fear us,
And we fear no dawning morrow,
Nor the grey wandering osprey Sorrow.'

The dance wound through the windless woods;
The ever-summered solitudes;
Until the tossing arms grew still
Upon the woody central hill;
And, gathered in a panting band,
We flung on high each waving hand,
And sang unto the starry broods.
In our raised eyes there flashed a glow
Of milky brightness to and fro
As thus our song arose: 'You stars,
Across your wandering ruby cars
Shake the loose reins: you slaves of God.
He rules you with an iron rod,
He holds you with an iron bond,
Each one woven to the other,
Each one woven to his brother
Like bubbles in a frozen pond;
But we in a lonely land abide

Unchainable as the dim tide,
With hearts that know nor law nor rule,
And hands that hold no wearisome tool,
Folded in love that fears no morrow,
Nor the grey wandering osprey Sorrow.'

O Patrick! for a hundred years
I chased upon that woody shore
The deer, the badger, and the boar.
O patrick! for a hundred years
At evening on the glimmering sands,
Beside the piled-up hunting spears,
These now outworn and withered hands
Wrestled among the island bands.
O patrick! for a hundred years
We went a-fishing in long boats
With bending sterns and bending bows,
And carven figures on their prows
Of bitterns and fish-eating stoats.
O patrick! for a hundred years
The gentle Niamh was my wife;
But now two things devour my life;
The things that most of all I hate:
Fasting and prayers.

—

S. Patrick. Tell on.

Oisin. Yes, yes,
For these were ancient Oisin's fate
Loosed long ago from Heaven's gate,
For his last days to lie in wait.
When one day by the tide I stood,
I found in that forgetfulness
Of dreamy foam a staff of wood
From some dead warrior's broken lance:
I tutned it in my hands; the stains
Of war were on it, and I wept,
Remembering how the Fenians stept
Along the blood-bedabbled plains,
Equal to good or grievous chance:
Thereon young Niamh softly came
And caught my hands, but spake no word
Save only many times my name,
In murmurs, like a frighted bird.
We passed by woods, and lawns of clover,
And found the horse and bridled him,
For we knew well the old was over.
I heard one say, 'His eyes grow dim
With all the ancient sorrow of men';
And wrapped in dreams rode out again

With hoofs of the pale findrinny
Over the glimmering purple sea.
Under the golden evening light,
The Immortals moved among thc fountains
By rivers and the woods' old night;
Some danced like shadows on the mountains
Some wandered ever hand in hand;
Or sat in dreams on the pale strand,
Each forehead like an obscure star
Bent down above each hooked knee,
And sang, and with a dreamy gaze
Watched where the sun in a saffron blaze
Was slumbering half in the sea-ways;
And, as they sang, the painted birds
Kept time with their bright wings and feet;
Like drops of honey came their words,
But fainter than a young lamb's bleat.

'An old man stirs the fire to a blaze,
In the house of a child, of a friend, of a brother.
He has over-lingered his welcome; the days,
Grown desolate, whisper and sigh to each other;
He hears the storm in the chimney above,
And bends to the fire and shakes with the cold,
While his heart still dreams of battle and love,

And the cry of the hounds on the hills of old.

But We are apart in the grassy places,
Where care cannot trouble the least of our days,
Or the softness of youth be gone from our faces,
Or love's first tenderness die in our gaze.
The hare grows old as she plays in the sun
And gazes around her with eyes of brightness;
Before the swift things that she dreamed of were done
She limps along in an aged whiteness;
A storm of birds in the Asian trees
Like tulips in the air a-winging,
And the gentle waves of the summer seas,
That raise their heads and wander singing,
Must murmur at last, "Unjust, unjust";
And "My speed is a weariness," falters the mouse,
And the kingfisher turns to a ball of dust,
And the roof falls in of his tunnelled house.
But the love-dew dims our eyes till the day
When God shall come from the Sea with a sigh
And bid the stars drop down from the sky,
And the moon like a pale rose wither away.'

II

Now, man of croziers, shadows called our names
And then away, away, like whirling flames;
And now fled by, mist-covered, without sound,
The youth and lady and the deer and hound;
'Gaze no more on the phantoms,' Niamh said,
And kissed my eyes, and, swaying her bright head
And her bright body, sang of faery and man
Before God was or my old line began;
Wars shadowy, vast, exultant; faeries of old
Who wedded men with rings of Druid gold;
And how those lovers never turn their eyes
Upon the life that fades and flickers and dies,
Yet love and kiss on dim shores far away
Rolled round with music of the sighing spray:
Yet sang no more as when, like a brown bee
That has drunk full, she crossed the misty sea
With me in her white arms a hundred years
Before this day; for now the fall of tears
Troubled her song.

I do not know if days
Or hours passed by, yet hold the morning rays
Shone many times among the glimmering flowers
Woven into her hair, before dark towers
Rose in the darkness, and the white surf gleamed
About them; and the horse of Faery screamed
And shivered, knowing the Isle of Many Fears,
Nor ceased until white Niamh stroked his ears
And named him by sweet names.

A foaming tide
Whitened afar with surge, fan-formed and wide,
Burst from a great door matred by many a blow
From mace and sword and pole-axe, long ago
When gods and giants warred. We rode between
The seaweed-covered pillars; and the green
And surging phosphorus alone gave light
On our dark pathway, till a countless flight
Of moonlit steps glimmered; and left and right
Dark statues glimmered over the pale tide
Upon dark thrones. Between the lids of one
The imaged meteors had flashed and run
And had disported in the stilly jet,
And the fixed stars had dawned and shone and set,

Since God made Time and Death and Sleep: the other
Stretched his long arm to where, a misty smother,
The stream churned, churned, and churned - his lips apart,
As though he told his never-slumbering heart
Of every foamdrop on its misty way.
Tying the horse to his vast foot that lay
Half in the unvesselled sea, we climbed the stair
And climbed so long, I thought the last steps were
Hung from the morning star; when these mild words
Fanned the delighted air like wings of birds:
'My brothers spring out of their beds at morn,
A-murmur like young partridge: with loud horn
They chase the noontide deer;
And when the dew-drowned stars hang in the air
Look to long fishing-lines, or point and pare
An ashen hunting spear.
O sigh, O fluttering sigh, be kind to me;
Flutter along the froth lips of the sea,
And shores the froth lips wet:
And stay a little while, and bid them weep:
Ah, touch their blue-veined eyelids if they sleep,
And shake their coverlet.
When you have told how I weep endlessly,
Flutter along the froth lips of the sea

And home to me again,
And in the shadow of my hair lie hid,
And tell me that you found a man unbid,
The saddest of all men.'

A lady with soft eyes like funeral tapers,
And face that seemed wrought out of moonlit vapours,
And a sad mouth, that fear made tremulous
As any ruddy moth, looked down on us;
And she with a wave-rusted chain was tied
To two old eagles, full of ancient pride,
That with dim eyeballs stood on either side.
Few feathers were on their dishevelled wings,
For their dim minds were with the ancient things.

'I bring deliverance,' pearl-pale Niamh said.

'Neither the living, nor the unlabouring dead,
Nor the high gods who never lived, may fight
My enemy and hope; demons for fright
Jabber and scream about him in the night;
For he is strong and crafty as the seas
That sprang under the Seven Hazel Trees,
And I must needs endure and hate and weep,
Until the gods and demons drop asleep,
Hearing Acdh touch thc mournful strings of gold.'

'Is he so dreadful?'
'Be not over-bold,
But fly while still you may.'
And thereon I:
'This demon shall be battered till he die,
And his loose bulk be thrown in the loud tide.'
'Flee from him,' pearl-pale Niamh weeping cried,
'For all men flee the demons'; but moved not
My angry king-remembering soul one jot.
There was no mightier soul of Heber's line;
Now it is old and mouse-like. For a sign
I burst the chain: still earless, neNeless, blind,
Wrapped in the things of the unhuman mind,
In some dim memory or ancient mood,
Still earless, netveless, blind, the eagles stood.

And then we climbed the stair to a high door;
A hundred horsemen on the basalt floor
Beneath had paced content: we held our way
And stood within: clothed in a misty ray
I saw a foam-white seagull drift and float
Under the roof, and with a straining throat
Shouted, and hailed him: he hung there a star,
For no man's cry shall ever mount so far;

Not even your God could have thrown down that hall;
Stabling His unloosed lightnings in their stall,
He had sat down and sighed with cumbered heart,
As though His hour were come.

We sought the part
That was most distant from the door; green slime
Made the way slippery, and time on time
Showed prints of sea-born scales, while down through it
The captive's journeys to and fro were writ
Like a small river, and where feet touched came
A momentary gleam of phosphorus flame.
Under the deepest shadows of the hall
That woman found a ring hung on the wall,
And in the ring a torch, and with its flare
Making a world about her in the air,
Passed under the dim doorway, out of sight,
And came again, holding a second light
Burning between her fingers, and in mine
Laid it and sighed: I held a sword whose shine
No centuries could dim, and a word ran
Thereon in Ogham letters, 'Manannan';
That sea-god's name, who in a deep content
Sprang dripping, and, with captive demons sent

Out of the sevenfold seas, built the dark hall
Rooted in foam and clouds, and cried to all
The mightier masters of a mightier race;
And at his cry there came no milk-pale face
Under a crown of thorns and dark with blood,
But only exultant faces.

Niamh stood
With bowed head, trembling when the white blade shone,
But she whose hours of tenderness were gone
Had neither hope nor fear. I bade them hide
Under the shadowS till the tumults died
Of the loud-crashing and earth-shaking fight,
Lest they should look upon some dreadful sight;
And thrust the torch between the slimy flags.
A dome made out of endless carven jags,
Where shadowy face flowed into shadowy face,
Looked down on me; and in the self-same place
I waited hour by hour, and the high dome,
Windowless, pillarless, multitudinous home
Of faces, waited; and the leisured gaze
Was loaded with the memory of days
Buried and mighty. When through the great door
The dawn came in, and glimmered on the floor

With a pale light, I journeyed round the hall
And found a door deep sunken in the wall,
The least of doors; beyond on a dim plain
A little mnnel made a bubbling strain,
And on the runnel's stony and bare edge
A dusky demon dry as a withered sedge
Swayed, crooning to himself an unknown tongue:
In a sad revelry he sang and swung
Bacchant and mournful, passing to and fro
His hand along the runnel's side, as though
The flowers still grew there: far on the sea's waste
Shaking and waving, vapour vapour chased,
While high frail cloudlets, fed with a green light,
Like drifts of leaves, immovable and bright,
Hung in the passionate dawn. He slowly turned:
A demon's leisure: eyes, first white, now burned
Like wings of kingfishers; and he arose
Barking. We trampled up and down with blows
Of sword and brazen battle-axe, while day
Gave to high noon and noon to night gave way;
And when he knew the sword of Manannan
Amid the shades of night, he changed and ran
Through many shapes; I lunged at the smooth throat
Of a great eel; it changed, and I but smote
A fir-tree roaring in its leafless top;

And thereupon I drew the livid chop
Of a drowned dripping body to my breast;
Horror from horror grew; but when the west
Had surged up in a plumy fire, I drave
Through heart and spine; and cast him in the wave
Lest Niamh shudder.

Full of hope and dread
Those two came carrying wine and meat and bread,
And healed my wounds with unguents out of flowers
That feed white moths by some De Danaan shrine;
Then in that hall, lit by the dim sea-shine,
We lay on skins of otters, and drank wine,
Brewed by the sea-gods, from huge cups that lay
Upon the lips of sea-gods in their day;
And then on heaped-up skins of otters slept.
And when the sun once more in saffron stept,
Rolling his flagrant wheel out of the deep,
We sang the loves and angers without sleep,
And all the exultant labours of the strong.
But now the lying clerics murder song
With barren words and flatteries of the weak.
In what land do the powerless turn the beak
Of ravening Sorrow, or the hand of Wrath?
For all your croziers, they have left the path

And wander in the storms and clinging snows,
Hopeless for ever: ancient Oisin knows,
For he is weak and poor and blind, and lies
On the anvil of the world.

S. Patrick. Be still: the skies
Are choked with thunder, lightning, and fierce wind,
For God has heard, and speaks His angry mind;
Go cast your body on the stones and pray,
For He has wrought midnight and dawn and day.

Oisin. Saint, do you weep? I hear amid the thunder
The Fenian horses; atmour torn asunder;
Laughter and cries. The armies clash and shock,
And now the daylight-darkening ravens flock.
Cease, cease, O mournful, laughing Fenian horn!

We feasted for three days. On the fourth morn
I found, dropping sea-foam on the wide stair,
And hung with slime, and whispering in his hair,
That demon dull and unsubduable;
And once more to a day-long battle fell,
And at the sundown threw him in the surge,
To lie until the fourth morn saw emerge
His new-healed shape; and for a hundred years
So watred, so feasted, with nor dreams nor fears,

Nor languor nor fatigue: an endless feast,
An endless war.

The hundred years had ceased;
I stood upon the stair: the surges bore
A beech-bough to me, and my heart grew sore,
Remembering how I had stood by white-haired Finn
Under a beech at Almhuin and heard the thin
Outcry of bats.

And then young Niamh came
Holding that horse, and sadly called my name;
I mounted, and we passed over the lone
And drifting greyness, while this monotone,
Surly and distant, mixed inseparably
Into the clangour of the wind and sea.

'I hear my soul drop down into decay,
And Mananna's dark tower, stone after stone.
Gather sea-slime and fall the seaward way,
And the moon goad the waters night and day,
That all be overthrown.

'But till the moon has taken all, I wage
War on the mightiest men under the skies,

And they have fallen or fled, age after age.
Light is man's love, and lighter is man's rage;
His purpose drifts and dies.'

And then lost Niamh murmured, 'Love, we go
To the Island of Forgetfulness, for lo!
The Islands of Dancing and of Victories
Are empty of all power.'

'And which of these
Is the Island of Content?'

'None know,' she said;
And on my bosom laid her weeping head.

III

Fled foam underneath us, and round us, a wandering and milky smoke,
High as the Saddle-girth, covering away from our glances the tide;
And those that fled, and that followed, from the foam-pale distance broke;
The immortal desire of Immortals we saw in their faces, and sighed.

I mused on the chase with the Fenians, and Bran, Sceolan, Lomair,
And never a song sang Niamh, and over my finger-tips
Came now the sliding of tears and sweeping of mist-cold hair,
And now the warmth of sighs, and after the quiver of lips.

Were we days long or hours long in riding, when, rolled in a grisly peace,
An isle lay level before us, with dripping hazel and oak?
And we stood on a sea's edge we saw not; for whiter than new-washed fleece
Fled foam underneath us, and round us, a wandering and milky smoke.

And we rode on the plains of the sea's edge; the sea's edge barren and grey,
Grey sand on the green of the grasses and over the dripping trees,
Dripping and doubling landward, as though they would hasten away,
Like an army of old men longing for rest from the moan of the seas.

But the trees grew taller and closer, immense in their wrinkling bark;
Dropping; a murmurous dropping; old silence and that one sound;
For no live creatures lived there, no weasels moved in the dark:

Long sighs arose in our spirits, beneath us bubbled the ground.

And the ears of the horse went sinking away in the hollow night,
For, as drift from a sailor slow drowning the gleams of the world and the sun,
Ceased on our hands and our faces, on hazel and oak leaf, the light,
And the stars were blotted above us, and the whole of the world was one.

Till the horse gave a whinny; for, cumbrous with stems of the hazel and oak,
A valley flowed down from his hoofs, and there in the long grass lay,
Under the starlight and shadow, a monstrous slumbering folk,
Their naked and gleaming bodies poured out and heaped in the way.

And by them were arrow and war-axe, arrow and shield and blade;
And dew-blanched horns, in whose hollow a child of three years old
Could sleep on a couch of rushes, and all inwrought and inlaid,
And more comely than man can make them with bronze and silver and gold.

And each of the huge white creatures was huger than four-score men;
The tops of their ears were feathered, their hands were the claws of birds,
And, shaking the plumes of the grasses and the leaves of the mural glen,
The breathing came from those bodies, long warless, grown whiter than curds.

The wood was so Spacious above them, that He who has stars for His flocks
Could fondle the leaves with His fingers, nor go from His dew-cumbered skies;
So long were they sleeping, the owls had builded their nests in their locks,
Filling the fibrous dimness with long generations of eyes.

And over the limbs and the valley the slow owls wandered and came,
Now in a place of star-fire, and now in a shadow-place wide;
And the chief of the huge white creatures, his knees in the soft star-flame,
Lay loose in a place of shadow: we drew the reins by his side.

Golden the nails of his bird-clawS, flung loosely along the dim ground;
In one was a branch soft-shining with bells more many than sighs

In midst of an old man's bosom; owls ruffling and pacing around
Sidled their bodies against him, filling the shade with their eyes.

And my gaze was thronged with the sleepers; no, not since the world began,
In realms where the handsome were many, nor in glamours by demons flung,
Have faces alive with such beauty been known to the salt eye of man,
Yet weary with passions that faded when the sevenfold seas were young.

And I gazed on the bell-branch, sleep's forebear, far sung by the Sennachies.
I saw how those slumbererS, grown weary, there camping in grasses deep,
Of wars with the wide world and pacing the shores of the wandering seas,
Laid hands on the bell-branch and swayed it, and fed of unhuman sleep.

Snatching the horn of Niamh, I blew a long lingering note.
Came sound from those monstrous sleepers, a sound like the stirring of flies.
He, shaking the fold of his lips, and heaving the pillar of his throat,
Watched me with mournful wonder out of the wells of his eyes.

I cried, 'Come out of the shadow, king of the nails of gold!
And tell of your goodly household and the goodly works of your hands,
That we may muse in the starlight and talk of the battles of old;
Your questioner, Oisin, is worthy, he comes from the Fenian lands.'

Half open his eyes were, and held me, dull with the smoke of their dreams;
His lips moved slowly in answer, no answer out of them came;
Then he swayed in his fingers the bell-branch, slow dropping a sound in faint streams
Softer than snow-flakes in April and piercing the marrow like flame.

Wrapt in the wave of that music, with weariness more than of earth,
The moil of my centuries filled me; and gone like a sea-covered stone
Were the memories of the whole of my sorrow and the memories of the whole of my mirth,
And a softness came from the starlight and filled me full to the bone.

In the roots of the grasses, the sorrels, I laid my body as low;
And the pearl-pale Niamh lay by me, her brow on the

midst of my breast;
And the horse was gone in the distance, and years after years 'gan flow;
Square leaves of the ivy moved over us, binding us down to our rest.

And, man of the many white croziers, a century there I forgot
How the fetlocks drip blocd in the battle, when the fallen on fallen lie rolled;
How the falconer follows the falcon in the weeds of the heron's plot,
And the name of the demon whose hammer made Conchubar's sword-blade of old.

And, man of the many white croziers, a century there I forgot
That the spear-shaft is made out of ashwood, the shield out of osier and hide;
How the hammers spring on the anvil, on the spearhead's burning spot;
How the slow, blue-eyed oxen of Finn low sadly at evening tide.

But in dreams, mild man of the croziers, driving the dust with their throngs,
Moved round me, of seamen or landsmen, all who are winter tales;
Came by me the kings of the Red Branch, with roaring of laughter and songs,

Or moved as they moved once, love-making or piercing the tempest with sails.

Came Blanid, Mac Nessa, tall Fergus who feastward of old time slunk,
Cook Barach, the traitor; and warward, the spittle on his beard never dry,
Dark Balor, as old as a forest, car-borne, his mighty head sunk
Helpless, men lifting the lids of his weary and death making eye.

And by me, in soft red raiment, the Fenians moved in loud streams,
And Grania, walking and smiling, sewed with her needle of bone.
So lived I and lived not, so wrought I and wrought not, with creatures of dreams,
In a long iron sleep, as a fish in the water goes dumb as a stone.

At times our slumber was lightened. When the sun was on silver or gold;
When brushed with the wings of the owls, in the dimness they love going by;
When a glow-worm was green on a grass-leaf, lured from his lair in the mould;
Half wakening, we lifted our eyelids, and gazed on the grass with a sigh.

So watched I when, man of the croziers, at the heel of a century fell,
Weak, in the midst of the meadow, from his miles in the midst of the air,
A starling like them that forgathered 'neath a moon waking white as a shell
When the Fenians made foray at morning with Bran, Sceolan, Lomair.

I awoke: the strange horse without summons out of the distance ran,
Thrusting his nose to my shoulder; he knew in his bosom deep
That once more moved in my bosom the ancient sadness of man,
And that I would leave the Immortals, their dimness, their dews dropping sleep.

O, had you seen beautiful Niamh grow white as the waters are white,
Lord of the croziers, you even had lifted your hands and wept:
But, the bird in my fingers, I mounted, remembering alone that delight
Of twilight and slumber were gone, and that hoofs impatiently stept.

I died, 'O Niamh! O white one! if only a twelve-houred day,
I must gaze on the beard of Finn, and move where the old

men and young
In the Fenians' dwellings of wattle lean on the chessboards and play,
Ah, sweet to me now were even bald Conan's slanderous tongue!

'Like me were some galley forsaken far off in Meridian isle,
Remembering its long-oared companions, sails turning to threadbare rags;
No more to crawl on the seas with long oars mile after mile,
But to be amid shooting of flies and flowering of rushes and flags.'

Their motionless eyeballs of spirits grown mild with mysterious thought,
Watched her those seamless faces from the valley's glimmering girth;
As she murmured, 'O wandering Oisin, the strength of the bell-branch is naught,
For there moves alive in your fingers the fluttering sadness of earth.

'Then go through the lands in the saddle and see what the mortals do,
And softly come to your Niamh over the tops of the tide;
But weep for your Niamh, O Oisin, weep; for if only your shoe

Brush lightly as haymouse earth's pebbles, you will come no more to my side.

'O flaming lion of the world, O when will you turn to your rest?'
I saw from a distant saddle; from the earth she made her moan:
'I would die like a small withered leaf in the autumn, for breast unto breast
We shall mingle no more, nor our gazes empty their sweetness lone

'In the isles of the farthest seas where only the spirits come.
Were the winds less soft than the breath of a pigeon who sleeps on her nest,
Nor lost in the star-fires and odours the sound of the sea's vague drum?
O flaming lion of the world, O when will you turn to your rest?'

The wailing grew distant; I rode by the woods of the wrinkling bark,
Where ever is murmurous dropping, old silence and that one sound;
For no live creatures live there, no weasels move in the dark:
In a reverie forgetful of all things, over the bubbling' ground.

And I rode by the plains of the sea's edge, where all is

barren and grey,
Grey sand on the green of the grasses and over the dripping trees,
Dripping and doubling landward, as though they would hasten away',
Like an army of old men longing for rest from the moan of the seas.

And the winds made the sands on the sea's edge turning and turning go,
As my mind made the names of the Fenians. Far from the hazel and oak,
I rode away on the surges, where, high aS the saddle-bow,
Fled foam underneath me, and round me, a wandering and milky smoke.

Long fled the foam-flakes around me, the winds fled out of the vast,
Snatching the bird in secret; nor knew I, embosomed apart,
When they froze the cloth on my body like armour riveted fast,
For Remembrance, lifting her leanness, keened in the gates of my heart.

Till, fattening the winds of the morning, an odour of new-mown hay
Came, and my forehead fell low, and my tears like berries fell down;
Later a sound came, half lost in the sound of a shore far away,

From the great grass-barnacle calling, and later the shore-weeds brown.

If I were as I once was, the strong hoofs crushing the sand and the shells,
Coming out of the sea as the dawn comes, a chaunt of love on my lips,
Not coughing, my head on my knees, and praying, and wroth with the bells,
I would leave no saint's head on his body from Rachlin to Bera of ships.

Making way from the kindling surges, I rode on a bridle-path
Much wondering to see upon all hands, of wattles and woodwork made,
Your bell-mounted churches, and guardless the sacred cairn and the mth,
And a small and a feeble populace stooping with mattock and spade,

Or weeding or ploughing with faces a-shining with much-toil wet;
While in this place and that place, with bodies unglorious, their chieftains stood,
Awaiting in patience the straw-death, croziered one, caught in your net:
Went the laughter of scorn from my mouth like the roaring of wind in a wood.

And before I went by them so huge and so speedy with eyes so bright,
Came after the hard gaze of youth, or an old man lifted his head:
And I rode and I rode, and I cried out, 'The Fenians hunt wolves in the night,
So sleep thee by daytime.' A voice cried, 'The Fenians a long time are dead.'

A whitebeard stood hushed on the pathway, the flesh of his face as dried grass,
And in folds round his eyes and his mouth, he sad as a child without milk-
And the dreams of the islands were gone, and I knew how men sorrow and pass,
And their hound, and their horse, and their love, and their eyes that glimmer like silk.

And wrapping my face in my hair, I murmured, 'In old age they ceased';
And my tears were larger than berries, and I murmured, 'Where white clouds lie spread
On Crevroe or broad Knockfefin, with many of old they feast
On the floors of the gods.' He cried, 'No, the gods a long time are dead.'

And lonely and longing for Niamh, I shivered and turned me about,
The heart in me longing to leap like a grasshopper into

her heart;
I turned and rode to the westward, and followed the sea's old shout
Till I saw where Maeve lies sleeping till starlight and midnight part.

And there at the foot of the mountain, two carried a sack full of sand,
They bore it with staggering and sweating, but fell with their burden at length.
Leaning down from the gem-studded saddle, I flung it five yards with my hand,
With a sob for men waxing so weakly, a sob for the Fenians' old strength.

The rest you have heard of, O croziered man; how, when divided the girth,
I fell on the path, and the horse went away like a summer fly;
And my years three hundred fell on me, and I rose, and walked on the earth,
A creeping old man, full of sleep, with the spittle on his beard never dry'.

How the men of the sand-sack showed me a church with its belfry in air;
Sorry place, where for swing of the war-axe in my dim eyes the crozier gleams;
What place have Caoilte and Conan, and Bran, Sceolan, Lomair?

Speak, you too are old with your memories, an old man surrounded with dreams.

S. Patrick. Where the flesh of the footsole clingeth on the burning stones is their place;
Where the demons whip them with wires on the burning stones of wide Hell,
Watching the blessed ones move far off, and the smile on God's face,
Between them a gateway of brass, and the howl of the angels who fell.

Oisin. Put the staff in my hands; for I go to the Fenians, O cleric, to chaunt
The war-songs that roused them of old; they will rise, making clouds with their Breath,
Innumerable, singing, exultant; the clay underneath them shall pant,
And demons be broken in pieces, and trampled beneath them in death.

And demons afraid in their darkness; deep horror of eyes and of wings,
Afraid, their ears on the earth laid, shall listen and rise up and weep;
Hearing the shaking of shields and the quiver of stretched bowstrings,
Hearing Hell loud with a murmur, as shouting and mocking we sweep.

We will tear out the flaming stones, and batter the gateway of brass
And enter, and none sayeth 'No' when there enters the strongly armed guest;
Make clean as a broom cleans, and march on as oxen move over young grass;
Then feast, making converse of wars, and of old wounds, and turn to our rest.

S. Patrick. On the flaming stones, without refuge, the limbs of the Fenians are tost;
None war on the masters of Hell, who could break up the world in their rage;
But kneel and wear out the flags and pray for your soul that is lost
Through the demon love of its youth and its godless and passionate age.

Oisin. Ah me! to be Shaken with coughing and broken with old age and pain,
Without laughter, a show unto children, alone with remembrance and fear;
All emptied of purple hours as a beggar's cloak in the rain,
As a hay-cock out on the flood, or a wolf sucked under a weir.

It were sad to gaze on the blessed and no man I loved of old there;
I throw down the chain of small stones! when life in my body has ceased,

I will go to Caoilte, and Conan, and Bran, Sceolan, Lomair,
And dwell in the house of the Fenians, be they in flames or at feast.

THE SONG OF THE HAPPY SHEPHERD

The woods of Arcady are dead,
And over is their antique joy;
Of old the world on dreaming fed;
Grey Truth is now her painted toy;
Yet still she turns her restless head:
But O, sick children of the world,
Of all the many changing things
In dreary dancing past us whirled,
To the cracked tune that Chronos sings,
Words alone are certain good.
Where are now the warring kings,
Word be-mockers? - By the Rood,
Where are now the watring kings?
An idle word is now their glory,
By the stammering schoolboy said,
Reading some entangled story:
The kings of the old time are dead;

The wandering earth herself may be
Only a sudden flaming word,
In clanging space a moment heard,
Troubling the endless reverie.
Then nowise worship dusty deeds,
Nor seek, for this is also sooth,
To hunger fiercely after truth,
Lest all thy toiling only breeds
New dreams, new dreams; there is no truth
Saving in thine own heart. Seek, then,
No learning from the starry men,
Who follow with the optic glass
The whirling ways of stars that pass -
Seek, then, for this is also sooth,
No word of theirs - the cold star-bane
Has cloven and rent their hearts in twain,
And dead is all their human truth.
Go gather by the humming sea
Some twisted, echo-harbouring shell.
And to its lips thy story tell,
And they thy comforters will be.
Rewording in melodious guile
Thy fretful words a little while,
Till they shall singing fade in ruth
And die a pearly brotherhood;
For words alone are certain good:

Sing, then, for this is also sooth.
I must be gone: there is a grave
Where daffodil and lily wave,
And I would please the hapless faun,
Buried under the sleepy ground,
With mirthful songs before the dawn.
His shouting days with mirth were crowned;
And still I dream he treads the lawn,
Walking ghostly in the dew,
Pierced by my glad singing through,
My songs of old earth's dreamy youth:
But ah! she dreams not now; dream thou!
For fair are poppies on the brow:
Dream, dream, for this is also sooth.

MAD AS THE MIST AND SNOW

Bolt and bar the shutter,
For the foul winds blow:
Our minds are at their best this night,
And I seem to know
That everything outside us is
Mad as the mist and snow.

Horace there by Homer stands,
Plato stands below,
And here is Tully's open page.
How many years ago
Were you and I unlettered lads
Mad as the mist and snow?

You ask what makes me sigh, old friend,
What makes me shudder so?
I shudder and I sigh to think
That even Cicero
And many-minded Homer were
Mad as the mist and snow.

THREE MARCHING SONGS

I

Remember all those renowned generations,
They left their bodies to fatten the wolves,
They left their homesteads to fatten the foxes,
Fled to far countries, or sheltered themselves
In cavern, crevice, or hole,
Defending Ireland's soul.

Be still, be still, what can be said?
My father sang that song,
But time amends old wrong,
All that is finished, let it fade.

Remember all those renowned generations,
Remember all that have sunk in their blood,
Remember all that have died on the scaffold,
Remember all that have fled, that have stood,
Stood, took death like a tune
On an old,tambourine.

Be still, be still, what can be said?
My father sang that song,
But time amends old wrong,
And all that's finished, let it fade.

Fail, and that history turns into rubbish,
All that great past to a trouble of fools;
Those that come after shall mock at O'Donnell,
Mock at the memory of both O'Neills,
Mock Emmet, mock Parnell,
All the renown that fell.

Be still, be still, what can be said?
My father sang that song,

but time amends old wrong,
And all that's finished, let it fade.

II

The soldier takes pride in saluting his Captain,
The devotee proffers a knee to his Lord,
Some back a mare thrown from a thoroughbred,,
Troy backed its Helen; Troy died and adored;
Great nations blossom above;
A slave bows down to a slave.

What marches through the mountain pass?
No, no, my son, not yet;
That is an airy spot,
And no man knows what treads the grass.

We know what rascal might has defiled,
The lofty innocence that it has slain,
Were we not born in the peasant's cot
Where men forgive if the belly gain?
More dread the life that we live,
How can the mind forgive?

What marches down the mountain pass?
No, no, my son, not yet;
That is an airy spot,
And no man knows what treads the grass.

What if there's nothing up there at the top?
Where are the captains that govern mankind?
What tears down a tree that has nothing within it?
A blast of the wind, O a marching wind,
March wind, and any old tune.
March, march, and how does it run?

What marches down the mountain pass?
No, no, my son, not yet;
That is an airy spot,
And no man knows what treads the grass.

III

Grandfather sang it under the gallows:
"Hear, gentlemen, ladies, and all mankind:
Money is good and a girl might be better,
But good strong blows are delights to the mind.'
There, standing on the cart,
He sang it from his heart.

Robbers had taken his old tambourine,
But he took down the moon
And rattled out a tunc;
Robbers had taken his old tambourinc.

"A girl I had, but she followed another,

Money I had, and it went in the night,
Strong drink I had, and it brought me to sorrow,
But a good strong cause and blows are delight.'
All there caught up the tune:
"Oh, on, my darling man.'

Robbers had taken his old tambourine,
But he took down the moon
And rattled out a tune;
Robbers had taken his old tambourine.

"Money is good and a girl might be better,
No matter what happens and who takes the fall,
But a good strong cause' - the rope gave a jerk there,
No more sang he, for his throat was too small;
But he kicked before he died,
He did it out of pride.

Robbers had taken his old tambourine,
But he took down the moon
And rattled out a tune;
Robbers had taken his old tambourine.

A WOMAN HOMER SUNG

If any man drew near
When I was young,
I thought, 'He holds her dear,'
And shook with hate and fear.
But O! 'twas bitter wrong
If he could pass her by
With an indifferent eye.

Whereon I wrote and wrought,
And now, being grey,
I dream that I have brought
To such a pitch my thought
That coming time can say,
'He shadowed in a glass
What thing her body was.'

For she had fiery blood
When I was young,
And trod so sweetly proud
As 'twere upon a cloud,

A woman Homer sung,
That life and letters seem
But an heroic dream.

TO A YOUNG BEAUTY

Dear fellow-artist, why so free
With every sort of company,
With every Jack and Jill?
Choose your companions from the best;
Who draws a bucket with the rest
Soon topples down the hill.

You may, that mirror for a school,
Be passionate, not bountiful
As common beauties may,
Who were not born to keep in trim
With old Ezekiel's cherubim
But those of Beauvarlet.

I know what wages beauty gives,
How hard a life her setvant lives,
Yet praise the winters gone:
There is not a fool can call me friend,

And I may dine at journey's end
With Landor and with Donne.

HE REMEMBERS FORGOTTEN BEAUTY

When my arms wrap you round I press
My heart upon the loveliness
That has long faded from the world;
The jewelled crowns that kings have hurled
In shadowy pools, when armies fled;
The love-tales wrought with silken thread
By dreaming ladies upon cloth
That has made fat the murderous moth;
The roses that of old time were
Woven by ladies in their hair,
The dew-cold lilies ladies bore
Through many a sacred corridor
Where such grey clouds of incense rose
That only God's eyes did not close:
For that pale breast and lingering hand
Come from a more dream-heavy land,
A more dream-heavy hour than this;
And when you sigh from kiss to kiss
I hear white Beauty sighing, too,

For hours when all must fade like dew.
But flame on flame, and deep on deep,
Throne over throne where in half sleep,
Their swords upon their iron knees,
Brood her high lonely mysteries.

THE BLESSED

Cumhal called out, bending his head,
Till Dathi came and stood,
With a blink in his eyes, at the cave-mouth,
Between the wind and the wood.

And Cumhal said, bending his knees,
'I have come by the windy way
To gather the half of your blessedness
And learn to pray when you pray.

'I can bring you salmon out of the streams
And heron out of the skies.'
But Dathi folded his hands and smiled
With the secrets of God in his eyes.

And Cumhal saw like a drifting smoke
All manner of blessed souls,

Women and children, young men with books,
And old men with croziers and stoles.

'praise God and God's Mother,' Dathi said,
'For God and God's Mother have sent
The blessedest souls that walk in the world
To fill your heart with content.'

'And which is the blessedest,' Cumhal said,
'Where all are comely and good?
Is it these that with golden thuribles
Are singing about the wood?'

'My eyes are blinking,' Dathi said,
'With the secrets of God half blind,
But I can see where the wind goes
And follow the way of the wind;

'And blessedness goes where the wind goes,
And when it is gone we are dead;
I see the blessedest soul in the world
And he nods a drunken head.

'O blessedness comes in the night and the day
And whither the wise heart knows;
And one has seen in the redness of wine
The Incorruptible Rose,

'That drowsily drops faint leaves on him
And the sweetness of desire,
While time and the world are ebbing away
In twilights of dew and of fire.'

SUPERNATURAL SONGS

I. Ribh at the Tomb of Baile and Aillinn

Because you have found me in the pitch-dark night
With open book you ask me what I do.
Mark and digest my tale, carry it afar
To those that never saw this tonsured head
Nor heard this voice that ninety years have cracked.
Of Baile and Aillinn you need not speak,
All know their tale, all know what leaf and twig,
What juncture of the apple and the yew,
Surmount their bones; but speak what none have heard.

The miracle that gave them such a death
Transfigured to pure substance what had once
Been bone and sinew; when such bodies join
There is no touching here, nor touching there,
Nor straining joy, but whole is joined to whole;
For the intercourse of angels is a light
Where for its moment both seem lost, consumed.

Here in the pitch-dark atmosphere above
The trembling of the apple and the yew,
Here on the anniversary of their death,
The anniversary of their first embrace,
Those lovers, purified by tragedy,
Hurry into each other's arms; these eyes,
By water, herb and solitary prayer
Made aquiline, are open to that light.
Though somewhat broken by the leaves, that light
Lies in a circle on the grass; therein
I turn the pages of my holy book.

II. Ribh denounces Patrick

An abstract Greek absurdity has crazed the man -
Recall that masculine Trinity. Man, woman, child (daughter or son),
That's how all natural or supernatural stories run.

Natural and supernatural with the self-same ring are wed.
As man, as beast, as an ephemeral fly begets, Godhead begets Godhead,
For things below are copies, the Great Smaragdine Tablet said.

Yet all must copy copies, all increase their kind;
When the conflagration of their passion sinks, damped by the body or the mind,

That juggling nature mounts, her coil in their embraces twined.

The mirror-scaled serpent is multiplicity,
But all that run in couples, on earth, in flood or air, share God that is but three,
And could beget or bear themselves could they but love as He.

III. Ribh in Ecstasy

What matter that you understood no word!
Doubtless I spoke or sang what I had heard
In broken sentences. My soul had found
All happiness in its own cause or ground.
Godhead on Godhead in sexual spasm begot
Godhead. Some shadow fell. My soul forgot
Those amorous cries that out of quiet come
And must the common round of day resume.

IV. There

There all the barrel-hoops are knit,
There all the serpent-tails are bit,
There all the gyres converge in one,
There all the planets drop in the Sun.

V. Ribh considers Christian Love insufficient

Why should I seek for love or study it?
It is of God and passes human wit.
I study hatred with great diligence,

For that's a passion in my own control,
A sort of besom that can clear the soul
Of everything that is not mind or sense.

Why do I hate man, woman or event?
That is a light my jealous soul has sent.
From terror and deception freed it can
Discover impurities, can show at last
How soul may walk when all such things are past,
How soul could walk before such things began.

Then my delivered soul herself shall learn
A darker knowledge and in hatred turn
From every thought of God mankind has had.
Thought is a garment and the soul's a bride
That cannot in that trash and tinsel hide:
Hatred of God may bring the soul to God.

At stroke of midnight soul cannot endure
A bodily or mental furniture.
What can she take until her Master give!
Where can she look until He make the show!
What can she know until He bid her know!
How can she live till in her blood He live!

VI. He and She

As the moon sidles up
Must she sidle up,

As trips the scared moon
Away must she trip:
'His light had struck me blind
Dared I stop".

She sings as the moon sings:
'I am I, am I;
The greater grows my light
The further that I fly.'
All creation shivers
With that sweet cry.

VII. What Magic Drum?

He holds him from desire, all but stops his breathing lest primordial Motherhood forsake his limbs, the child no longer rest,
Drinking joy as it were milk upon his breast.

Through light-obliterating garden foliage what magic drum?
Down limb and breast or down that glimmering belly move his mouth and sinewy tongue.
What from the forest came? What beast has licked its young?

VIII. Whence had they come?

Eternity is passion, girl or boy
Cry at the onset of their sexual joy
'For ever and for ever'; then awake

Ignorant what Dramatis personae spake;
A passion-driven exultant man sings out
Sentences that he has never thought;
The Flagellant lashes those submissive loins
Ignorant what that dramatist enjoins,
What master made the lash. Whence had they come,
The hand and lash that beat down frigid Rome?
What sacred drama through her body heaved
When world-transforming Charlemagne was conceived?

IX. The Four Ages of Man

He with body waged a fight,
But body won; it walks upright.
Then he struggled with the heart;
Innocence and peace depart.
Then he struggled with the mind;
His proud heart he left behind.
Now his wars on God begin;
At stroke of midnight God shall win.

X. Conjunctions

If Jupiter and Saturn meet,
What a cop of mummy wheat!

The sword's a cross; thereon He died:
On breast of Mars the goddess sighed.

XI. A Needle's Eye

All the stream that's roaring by
Came out of a needle's eye;
Things unborn, things that are gone,
From needle's eye still goad it on.

XII. Meru

Civilisation is hooped together, brought
Under a mle, under the semblance of peace
By manifold illusion; but man's life is thought,
And he, despite his terror, cannot cease
Ravening through century after century,
Ravening, raging, and uprooting that he may come
Into the desolation of reality:
Egypt and Greece, good-bye, and good-bye, Rome!
Hermits upon Mount Meru or Everest,
Caverned in night under the drifted snow,
Or where that snow and winter's dreadful blast
Beat down upon their naked bodies, know
That day brings round the night, that before dawn
His glory and his monuments are gone.